# FIVE REASONS WHY WE LOVE THIS BOOK:

CHAOS is bound to kick off when Creature's about!

Creature beats all the competition, no contest!

Winning illustrations!

The JOKES are in a LEAGUE of their own!

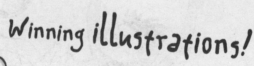

FAAAAAA

# A sneaky peek of what's inside!

'Eeeeeeeeeeeeeeeek!!!!' The marshals dropped the bag, which burst open, knocking Alexis back in a thundering avalanche of footballs. Behind her, Karl and Woodstock went skittering as a wave of balls rolled under their feet. Jake dodged the balls and made a lunge towards Creature.

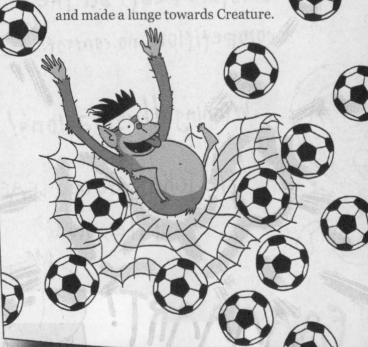

'Ow!' Pain shot through Jake's ankle, and he stumbled to a halt. Creature bounced gleefully onto the pitch and headed for the goal, where a player was about to take a free kick. A line of defenders stood in front of him, waiting for the whistle.

The ref sucked in his breath, ready to blow.

Creature bounced up to him and grabbed the whistle out of his mouth.

Pheeeeeeeeeeeeeeeep!

For Isaac, already a football legend—S.W.

For Lizzie, Sarah and all the brilliant
team at OUP—D.O'C.

# OXFORD
UNIVERSITY PRESS

Great Clarendon Street, Oxford OX2 6DP

Oxford University Press is a department of the University of Oxford.
It furthers the University's objective of excellence in research, scholarship,
and education by publishing worldwide. Oxford is a registered trade mark of
Oxford University Press in the UK and in certain other countries

British Library Cataloguing in Publication Data available

Data available

rec                                                                 sts.

# CREATURE TEACHER

## OUT TO WIN

SAM WATKINS and
ILLUSTRATED BY David O'Connell

OXFORD
UNIVERSITY PRESS

# CHAPTER 1

## BANANAS LOSE APPEAL FOR BARNABY

'What on EARTH is Barnaby wearing?' Jake said to Alexis.

Barnaby, their classmate, was standing near the gate to Bembley Road Sports Club, wearing a strange yellow and black outfit that went over his head, ending in a pointy hood. Underneath, he had a face like he'd just eaten a mouthful of mouldy cabbage soup.

'Dunno,' Alexis said, giggling. 'He's not happy about it, though . . .'

As they reached Barnaby, Jake realized it was a banana costume.

'If you laugh, I'll never speak to you again,' Barnaby growled. 'Ever.'

Jake tried not to laugh. 'OK, I won't—but why are you dressed as a banana?'

Barnaby pointed. '*That's* why.'

Not far off, Jake saw a stall with a sign reading:

## BURT'S BANANA SMOOTHIES

Sponsors of the County Five-A-Side
Junior League Football Tournament

'That company have put loads of money into the tournament,' said Barnaby, bitterly. 'So Mrs Blunt decided it would be great to have all the marshals dress up as bananas, to promote them. Our headteacher's evilness knows no bounds!'

'Oh, so Mrs Blunt made you a marshal, then?' asked Jake.

'No, I volunteered. But I didn't know I'd have to wear a stupid fruit costume,' snarled the angry banana.

Alexis couldn't keep a straight face any longer. 'Ha ha! Oh, Barnaby, that's such bad luck! I'd never be seen dead in a banana costume . . .'

A snigger from behind Jake made him turn around. Amelia Trotter-Hogg, Pony-tailed Pest of Class 5a, was standing there, a look of evil glee on her face.

'For once, I agree with Alexis,' Amelia said, smirking, and then turned to Barnaby. 'I thought this was a football tournament, not a fruit and veg competition.'

'What are you doing here?' said Alexis, coldly. 'I thought you had Prissypants' Pony Club on Saturdays.'

Amelia glared. 'It's *Priscilla's* Pony Club, actually.' She turned to go, then looked back. 'And you'll find out why I'm here in a bit . . .'

She marched off. Barnaby glared after her.

'It's her fault I'm dressed like this! I'd have been on the team with you guys if she hadn't told on me.'

'You can't blame Amelia,' Alexis said. 'You're the one who put slugs in her lunchbox. You should have known it would get you a day's work on the Rockery—it was just bad luck that was the day they picked the team.'

A day's work on the Rockery was the punishment for any pupil getting three Sad Faces. A Sad Face was given for breaking a school rule. There were a hundred and forty-one (or maybe two) school rules, so it was quite easy to break one without even knowing you had, and Barnaby found it easier than most.

'Jake! Alexis!'

Woodstock was walking towards them, with a little old man dressed from head to toe in

football gear. The old man's face was painted in blue and white stripes, their team colours, and he was wearing a bobble hat to match. He held a megaphone to his mouth.

'WE'RE ON OUR WAY TO BEMBLEY, WE'RE GONNA MISS ASSEMBLY, DA DAAA DAAA DA! DA DAAA DAAA DA!'

Woodstock rolled his eyes.

'Stop it, Grandad!' He turned to the others. 'My grandad's bonkers about football. In fact, he's just plain bonkers. Grandad, these are my friends . . .'

'SPEAK UP, LAD!' Grandad bellowed into the megaphone. Jake's eardrums quivered painfully.

'I said—these are my friends, Jake and Alexis!' Woodstock yelled in his ear.

'No need to shout,' Grandad said. 'I'm not deaf.'

Grandad shook Jake's and Alexis's hands, then turned to Barnaby.

'And who's this?'

'Oh—hi, Barnaby,' Woodstock said, recognizing Barnaby for the first time. 'Sorry, I didn't recognize you in that costume. Grandad, this is Barnaby . . .'

'Hello Bananaby,' Grandad said, cheerfully.

Alexis stifled a giggle. Barnaby's face went more strawberry than banana-coloured.

'BAR-NA-BY!' shouted Woodstock. 'Oh, never mind. Barnaby, can you help my grandad find a seat? We have to go and get changed now.'

Barnaby sighed as Grandad took his arm,

chatting away merrily. 'Thank you, Bananaby . . .
unusual name, is it Scandinavian?'

He dragged Barnaby off into the crowd. Jake
shook his head. 'Poor old Bananaby . . . I mean
Barnaby.'

Woodstock grinned. 'Trust my grandad to
come up with that one! Yeah, he really wanted
to be on the team, didn't he—'

'Look, never mind him,' Alexis interrupted.
'What's important is that we win the Golden
Ball trophy. We did really well in the qualifying
rounds—plus we've done loads of extra training.
As Mr Hyde always says: what are we?'

'Winners!' Jake and Woodstock said,
laughing, but a sudden pang of worry hit
Jake at the mention of their teacher. It was
common knowledge that Mr Hyde was the

Best Teacher in the Universe. *Not* such common knowledge was that he had an unfortunate habit of turning into a very naughty and chaos-creating creature when he got stressed or over-excited.

'Let's hope Mr Hyde doesn't turn into Creature today,' he said. 'We won't be winners then—we'll be in big trouble!'

'We'll just have to make sure he keeps as calm as possible,' said Alexis. 'He was sorting out the new kits—he said he'd take them up to the changing rooms in the club house.'

'Let's go then,' Woodstock said. 'We've only got about twenty minutes till the first match.'

As they ploughed through the crowd, heading for the club house, Jake had a niggling feeling that something was wrong. Then he remembered something Amelia had said. 'You'll find out why I'm here in a bit.' *What had she meant by that?*

'Uh oh. Something's up.' Woodstock pointed.

In front of the club house, Jake saw a small crowd of people. Their two classmates, Nora and Karl, were there. Facing them was the Pony-tailed Pest, Amelia Trotter-Hogg.

Even worse luck, next to Amelia stood Mrs Blunt. She was dressed in a very sharp suit and huge sunglasses, and was leaning towards Nora and Karl like a praying mantis about to strike.

# CHAPTER 2

## KIT CATASTROPHE CAUSES CHAOS!

Jake, Alexis, and Woodstock ran up beside Nora.

'What's happening?' Jake asked her in a low voice. 'Why is Amelia here?'

'Amelia is now playing on our team,' Nora said, through gritted teeth.

'What? Why?' Alexis demanded.

Mrs Blunt leaned forward. 'Rona was injured in a match yesterday and is unable to play today. So I have decided to put Amelia on the team in her place.'

'But that's ridiculous!' Alexis cried. 'One of the substitutes should play! Ralph—or Oliver. They've been to all the training sessions. Amelia hasn't been to a single one!'

'We've got a watertight game plan,' Nora added, tapping her clipboard importantly. 'Any change in line-up is going to cause major problems.'

Amelia squinted at the clipboard.

'What are all those numbers and scribbles? That's maths, not football! Stick to what you're good at, boring N—' She shot a glance at Mrs Blunt and stopped.

Nora looked as though she was about to whack Amelia with the watertight game plan. Karl and Jake grabbed her.

'Don't, Nora,' Jake muttered.

Mrs Blunt's mouth twisted into what Jake imagined she thought was a smile, but looked more like a shark getting ready to bite your legs off.

'So, it's settled. Amelia will replace Rona as deputy captain,' Mrs Blunt said. 'Now, if you'll excuse me, I have more important things to attend to.'

She stalked away.

Alexis, Nora, Karl, Jake, and Woodstock looked at each other, then at Amelia.

Amelia gave them a gleeful smirk.

Alexis's face went purple with rage. 'I'm team captain, and I'm not—'

'Halloooo! What's going on?'

Jake looked up to see Mr Hyde bouncing towards them. He was wearing a blue tracksuit, fluorescent orange trainers, and a sweatband that made his hair stick up like a startled porcupine. Over his shoulder hung a large kitbag.

Alexis ran to him. 'Sir, Mrs Blunt says Amelia has to play in Rona's place. It'll mess everything up!'

Mr Hyde scratched his head. He looked at Amelia, who suddenly managed to look sorry for herself.

'Come now,' Mr Hyde said. 'One banana does not a fruit salad make.'

Everyone looked blank.

'Sorry, sir?' Jake asked, confused. He had a sudden shock of fear that Mr Hyde was changing into Creature. Sometimes he said odd things just before he changed. Jake looked quickly at his teacher but Mr Hyde looked quite relaxed and not at all like he was about to disappear in a puff of smoke.

'Bananas aren't great in fruit salad,' said Nora. 'They go all brown and slimy—'

'Forget the fruit salad thing,' Mr Hyde said, quickly. 'I meant that it doesn't matter *who's* on the team, it's about everyone *working together* as a team. Alexis, as captain, it's your job to make sure they do—'

Just then, a crackle came over a loudspeaker.

'TEN MINUTES TO KICK-OFF! ALL TEAMS TO PITCH SIDE, PLEASE!'

Alexis gasped. 'We're not even changed yet! Sir, have you got the kits?'

Mr Hyde hoisted the kitbag off his shoulder and unzipped it. Inside was a stack of brand new kits, each in a clear plastic wrapper. He handed each pupil a kit, and they all raced into the club house lobby. Alexis and Amelia disappeared into the girls' changing room; Jake, Karl, and Woodstock went into the boys'.

Jake tore the wrapper off his kit and pulled the shirt over his head. Woodstock and Karl did the same.

They looked at each other.

'What's happened to our kits?' Woodstock exclaimed.

Jake looked down at himself. His shirt was shiny and new, and white and blue . . . and came down to his knees!

No one spoke. Then Jake heard a muffled shriek from next door. They all ran back into the lobby, at the same time as Alexis and Amelia burst out of the other door. Their shirts, too, looked more like big, baggy dresses. They all stared at each other.

'These are adult kits!' Alexis cried.

'Clever Mr Hyde must have picked up the wrong ones,' Amelia growled.

Jake held up his shorts. They were so huge he'd fit into one leg.

'We can't play in these—' he began. At that moment, a voice boomed out from a speaker on the wall.

'FIVE MINUTES TO KICK-OFF. ALL PLAYERS REPORT TO THEIR PITCHES IMMEDIATELY.'

Karl groaned. 'Now what?'

Alexis took a deep breath. 'We'll have to wear them for this match. We've got to play in matching kits—they won't let us play otherwise.'

Everyone trooped back into the changing rooms. Jake managed to tie his tent-like shorts on, but they were very loose. He waddled back outside just as Alexis's head poked around the girls' changing room door.

'You guys go on ahead! I'll meet you there in a sec—I need the toilet!'

'Yeah, me too,' Jake heard Amelia say.

The boys ran out of the club house and dodged through the crowd to the pitches, shirts billowing out behind them like parachutes.

'Where's our pitch?' puffed Karl. Jake peered around, then saw Mr Hyde standing with a referee, waving at them frantically from beside

one of the pitches.

'Here they are,' said Mr Hyde, as they ran up.
He stared at Jake in surprise.

'Why are you wearing long dresses?'

'They're extra-large adult kits, sir,' Jake panted.

'You must have bought the wrong ones.'

Mr Hyde slapped his head. 'Botheration!

I was in such a hurry this morning. I'll phone the shop and get someone to bring the right ones.'

He turned to the referee. 'Can they play in their normal clothes for now?'

The referee shook his head, sternly. 'Teams must be in matching kits.' He turned to Jake. 'Where's the rest of your team?'

Jake looked back towards the club house. He could see Amelia picking her way towards them, but Alexis was nowhere in sight.

'Where's Alexis?' Jake asked, as Amelia sauntered up. 'The game's about to start!'

Amelia shrugged. 'I don't know. She went to the toilet, then disappeared. She must have chickened out and run off!'

# CHAPTER 3

## TEAM RALLIES
## DESPITE COLOSSAL
## SHORTS SHAMBLES

Everyone gaped at Amelia.

Nora snorted. 'Rubbish! Alexis would never miss a football game.'

'We have to find her!' Woodstock exclaimed.

The referee shook his head. 'No time. We've got to start the match.'

He marched onto the pitch, followed by the other team who stared at Jake's team in their huge, baggy kits and nudged each other, giggling.

Amelia glared at them.

'What are you staring at?' she snapped. 'Never seen real talent before? OK team, follow me.'

'You can't boss us around,' Karl said.

Amelia smirked. 'Actually, I can. Mrs Blunt made me deputy captain, so now Alexis isn't here, *I'm* captain.'

It was true. There was nothing Jake and the rest of the team could do except trudge after Amelia.

'HEY! WAIT!'

Jake turned. 'Alexis!'

Alexis was racing towards them, her shirt flapping wildly.

'What happened to you?!' Jake asked, relieved, as she skidded up.

'The toilet door stuck,' Alexis panted. 'It must have jammed. I called and called, but everyone had gone! I had to climb out of the window.'

'Captains, please!' called the ref. Amelia sulkily stepped back to let Alexis take her place for the coin-toss, then everyone ran to their positions.

Jake was playing in defence, with Amelia. As he took his position, he saw Nora, Mr Hyde, and Woodstock's grandad standing at the side of the pitch. Mr Hyde was talking on a mobile phone and looking a bit stressed.

The whistle went.

Pheeeeeeeeeeeeeeeep!

*Game on!* The captain of the other team slammed the ball towards a player near Jake. Jake tried to get a toe to it, but his shorts slipped down, catching his foot and sending him flying. Scrambling up, he saw the player dribbling the ball towards their goal, where Karl was crouched down, ready—but where was Amelia?!

'SMILE, DARLING!'

To Jake's astonishment, he saw Amelia

striking a pose for her mum, who was standing on the sideline, taking a photograph. She didn't see the enemy striker dribble the ball neatly round her and slam it straight towards the goal.

Karl prepared to dive for it, and, as he did so, his shorts fell down. Flushing, he bent to pull them up, and the ball whizzed over his head.

'GOAL!!!!!!' whooped the goal-scorer, amidst cheers from the crowd. Jake ran over to Amelia.

'AMELIA! What were you doing?'

She tossed her head. 'I wasn't doing anything!'

'Exactly—' Jake began, but the ref was waving them back to positions.

*Pheeeeeeeeeeeeeep!*

Still furious with Amelia, Jake kept his eye on her but this made him miss a couple of easy tackles. *Focus on the ball,* Jake told himself firmly, hitching up his shorts for the umpteenth time. He saw it whizz towards their goal again and gave chase, but, just as he was nearly on it, Alexis appeared out of nowhere and whisked the ball away. She flew back up the left flank, shirt billowing, dodging defenders.

'To me!' Woodstock yelled from centre

field, but Alexis ignored him and took the shot. Jake shook his head. It was going wide—but wait, Woodstock was there, lolloping towards the airborne ball, trying desperately to hold his shorts up . . . It was no good, they were going . . . going—gone! The shorts dropped to his ankles, tripping him forward, and, as he fell, his head whacked the ball into the net, catching the goalie completely by surprise. Woodstock looked up from the ground, rubbing his head.

'W-what happened?' he asked, dazed.

'GOOOOOOOOOAL!!!!!' Jake bellowed, racing down the pitch to leap on Woodstock.

'THERE'S ONLY ONE WOODSTOCK STONE!' bawled Woodstock's grandad, and fell off his chair in excitement.

As the whistle blew for half-time, Alexis called everyone round.

'We've got to keep the pressure on,' she said. 'Pass the ball to me whenever you can.'

Nora frowned. 'It's about teamwork, Alexis.'

'Whatever. I mean, yes, of course. Come on team, I—I mean we—can do this!'

As the second half got underway Jake tried to do as Alexis had asked, but the other team were marking her closely. No one could get the ball near her. With five minutes to go Jake saw his chance. He dodged a defender just outside the box and looked round for Alexis.

'Take the shot, Jake!' shouted Nora. 'A thirty-degree angle should do it!'

Taking a deep breath, Jake fired, watching the ball sail towards the net almost as if in slow motion . . .

THWACK! Someone rammed into him from behind! As he flew forward, he caught a glimpse of the ball whizzing into the top corner of the goal, missing the goalie's fingertips by millimetres.

Then, CRACK! He hit the ground, his ankle twisting painfully under him.

Jake heard a roaring that could have been the crowd, or his ears ringing . . . he rolled over, trying to catch his breath, pain stabbing through his ankle.

'Stretcher!' he heard someone shout.

*Stretcher?!* 'No—I'm all right,' Jake panted. He staggered dizzily to his feet.

'Are you sure?' Woodstock looked worried. Jake waved him away.

'I'm fine!' *There's no way I'm being stretchered off now!* he thought.

The last minutes of the game were a blur to Jake. As the final whistle blew, he heaved a sigh of relief. His ankle was throbbing badly, but it was worth it—they were through to the semi-finals!

Jake limped to meet the others as a storm of cheering burst from the crowd. Amelia ran back to her parents to pose for more photos.

On the sideline, Woodstock's grandad was singing lustily into his megaphone, while Nora shouted something in his ear. Next to them, Mr Hyde was grinning like a Cheshire cat, waving a scarf over his head, and steaming.

Jake grinned and started to wave back. Then he stopped.

*Steaming?* Jake squinted across the pitch at his teacher. Steam was pouring off Mr Hyde like he was a boiling kettle. And his face was a livid red . . .

'NOOOOO!!' Jake gasped.

FAAAAAAAAAAAAAARRRRRT!

Wheeeeeeee . . . . . . . . . . . .

POP! POP! POP!

BANG!

# CHAPTER 4

## CREATURE CAUSES QUARTER-FINAL CHAOS!

A super-loud fart noise ripped through the air. Screaming people flung themselves to the ground as a cloud of purple smoke engulfed them. As the smoke began to clear, Jake saw that the only person left upright was Woodstock's grandad. He peered at the people cowering around him on the ground, a puzzled look on his face.

'Grandad! I told him not to bring those smoke bombs!' Woodstock groaned.

'That was no smoke bomb!' Jake exclaimed. 'That was Mr Hyde changing into Creature!'

'Oh no!' Alexis took off towards the sideline, followed by Woodstock and Karl. Jake limped after them to where Mr Hyde had been standing a few moments before. Woodstock's grandad peered at them as they approached.

'Oh, it's you, Woody. I think I just farted a proper stinker,' he said. 'Must have been that prune juice I had this morning . . .'

'Why do you drink that stuff? It always gives you wind,' Woodstock said, his eyes darting round, trying to spot Creature. Nora crawled out from under a chair, coughing.

'Mr Hyde . . . Creature . . .' she managed to choke out.

Jake grabbed her. 'Nora! Where did he go?'

Catching her breath, Nora pointed. Through the clearing smoke Jake saw a small, furry shape bouncing away. He was still wearing the sweatband round his head, making him look like a cross between a tennis player from the 1980s and a gorilla that had shrunk in the wash.

'After him!' Nora, Woodstock, Karl, and Alexis ran after Creature, with Jake limping painfully along behind. Jake saw Creature bounce over a man who was picking himself up off the ground, nearly knocking his hat off. The man gaped, then ducked as Alexis and the others all leapt over him too. He rubbed his eyes.

'Did you see that? Looked like some kind of monkey!' the man exclaimed, as Jake hobbled up.

Jake thought quickly.

'Oh no, that's just our, um . . . team mascot,' he said. 'He got over-excited . . .'

'He's heading for the next pitch!' shouted Karl from up ahead. 'The game's still going on!'

Alexis put on an extra spurt of energy and hurled herself towards Creature as he reached the sideline. At that moment, two banana-clad marshals staggered in front of him, carrying between them a huge net bag full of footballs. As Alexis sprang forward to grab him, Creature took a flying leap and landed slap bang on top of the bag.

'KIPPER!' Creature squawked.

'Eeeeeeeeeeeeeeek!!!!' The marshals dropped the bag, which burst open, knocking Alexis back in a thundering avalanche of footballs. Behind her, Karl and Woodstock went skittering as a wave of balls rolled under their feet. Jake dodged the balls and made a lunge towards Creature.

'Ow!' Pain shot through Jake's ankle, and he stumbled to a halt. Creature bounced gleefully onto the pitch and headed for the goal, where a player was about to take a free kick. A line of defenders stood in front of him, waiting for the whistle.

The ref sucked in his breath, ready to blow.

Creature bounced up to him and grabbed the whistle out of his mouth.

Pheeeeeeeeeeeeeeep! Creature gave it a healthy blast, right in the astonished ref's face.

Facing the other way, the player taking the kick didn't see what had happened, but on the whistle he started his run-up for the ball. Just as he kicked it, Creature launched himself

45

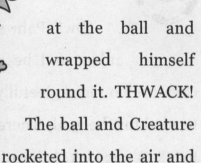

at the ball and wrapped himself round it. THWACK! The ball and Creature rocketed into the air and somersaulted over the line of defenders towards the goal . . .

'KIPPPPPPPPPPERRRRRRRRRRRRR!'

The goalie saw Creature spinning towards him like a demented Catherine wheel, and threw himself, cowering, to the ground. Jake watched, open-mouthed, as ball and Creature shot over the top of the net and landed—SQUIDGE!—in a large vat of tomato ketchup on a hotdog stand. Creature's surprised head appeared over the side, almost entirely covered in ketchup.

'We can catch him now!' Karl cried to the others. They started picking their way through the crowd of perplexed spectators along the sideline. Jake tried to keep up, but every step was agony, plus his shorts kept falling down. It was no good—he had to stop. Nora saw him and ran back.

'Jake? Are you OK?'

He swallowed. 'I-I'll be all right . . .'

Nora looked round. 'Look, why don't we go to the club house café? It's just over there.'

Jake looked anxiously after the others, but his ankle twinged again.

He grimaced. 'OK. But you go . . .'

'No. I'm staying with you.'

Nora helped Jake across to the café. He sat down at a table and stared moodily out of the window while Nora went to fetch two banana smoothies. *This whole thing is my fault*, he thought. He should have kept more of an eye on Mr Hyde, and he shouldn't have got himself injured, because now he couldn't even help to catch Creature.

A loud voice made him turn.

'HURRY UP GIRL!' Mrs Blunt was standing behind Nora in the queue. She was with a man carrying a large camera—the reporter from the local paper, Jake realized.

Mrs Blunt tapped angrily on the counter and snapped at the girl serving Nora.

'Come along, I haven't got all day . . .'

Jake rolled his eyes. Whoever had taught Mrs Blunt manners hadn't done a very good job! He looked out of the window again, and noticed Amelia talking to one of the banana-clad marshals. The marshal handed her a kitbag, and she disappeared off in the direction of the club house entrance. As the marshal turned, Jake saw that it was Barnaby.

'What's going on out there?' Nora had come back with the drinks.

'I think our proper kits have—' Jake began, but at that moment, a door banged loudly behind him. He saw Nora's eyes widen, and she nearly spat her smoothie out.

'Oh no! Guess who's here . . .'

# CHAPTER 5

## HEAD SPLATTED IN MILKSHAKE SHOCKER!

Jake whirled round. In the doorway stood Creature, wild-eyed and dripping crimson globs of ketchup all over the floor. He looked like something out of a horror movie. People at the tables nearest him jumped up, open-mouthed in shock.

'What *is* it?' someone yelled.

Jake and Nora pushed their way through

tables towards him.

'It's OK,' Jake called, raising his hands for calm. 'He's our team mascot...'

'He's covered in blood!' a woman near them said, hands over her mouth. 'Someone should call an ambulance!'

'It's only tomato ketchup,' Nora reassured her.

Creature saw Jake and Nora approaching and started to back out towards the door when it burst open again. Alexis ran in, Karl and Woodstock behind her.

'Squaaaaaaaark!'

Cornered, Creature's eyes darted round. He spotted a table where a couple was sitting. Without warning, he shot sideways and leapt onto it, landing with a crash in the woman's plate of fish and chips.

The woman threw herself backwards, as chips flew in all directions.

'What the—' The man tried to grab him, but the now chip-covered Creature grabbed a fork and pole-vaulted himself onto to the next table, crash-landing between two large chocolate ice creams. The two girls sitting at the table sprang up in fright, as Creature grabbed both ice creams, and tipped them noisily into his throat.

'Mmmmm!' He wiped a chocolate moustache

from his lips.

'Grab him now,' Jake whispered to Karl, who was closest to Creature.

Karl tiptoed up behind Creature . . . but Creature turned and saw him.

'B∪∪∪∪∪∪∪∪∪∪∪∪∪∪∪∪RP!!!!'

A loud, chocolatey burp erupted from his mouth.

'Ugh!' Karl jumped back, as Creature boinged off.

'Excuse us . . .' Jake skidded round the panicked girls after Creature. He was heading towards a corner table, slightly hidden behind a chocolate vending machine. When he saw who was sitting at the table, Jake skidded to a halt and jumped behind the machine.

'Mrs Blunt!' he hissed.

Nora, Woodstock, Karl, and Alexis ducked behind a table. Jake peeked out. Mrs Blunt was sitting opposite the reporter, who was holding his camera up, ready to take a picture of her. Neither saw Creature skittering across the floor towards them, leaving a sticky trail of ketchup, chips, and chocolate ice cream in his wake . . .

'Smile!' the reporter was saying.

'I *am* smiling,' Mrs Blunt said, pulling her usual sharky grimace.

'Um . . . maybe try a different smile? More, I dunno, *cheerful* . . .'

The reporter's voice trailed away. Jake saw his face freeze into an image of petrified horror, as Creature's ketchuppy, chip-covered head slowly rose up over Mrs Blunt's left shoulder, his eyes fixed greedily on the large strawberry milkshake that sat on the table in front of her.

Mrs Blunt saw the reporter's look of terror.

'My smile isn't that bad—' The words froze on her lips, as a soggy, sticky paw was planted on her shoulder. She turned, very slowly . . .

'AAAAARGGHHHHHHH!!!!!' Mrs Blunt howled.

'ΛΛΛRRRRR-ΛΛH-ΛH-ΛΛH-ARRRRRRRR!!!' Creature howled, louder and more Tarzan-like. Still howling, he vaulted over Mrs Blunt's shoulder, snatched her milkshake off the table, and made a wild Tarzanesque leap straight up towards a ceiling light. He managed to grab the light with one paw, but he couldn't keep the milkshake glass upright. Jake watched in fascinated horror as the glass tipped further and further over, until the contents of the glass poured in a thick, pink waterfall—SPLOSH!—onto Mrs Blunt's head.

The reporter stared at Mrs Blunt. Mrs Blunt stared at the reporter, a slimy pink river

flowing down her nose and
dripping off her chin. She
wiped some of it away and
stared at it as though it was
alien snot.

'Eurrrrrgh,' she said, and
then slowly slumped forward
in a dead faint, into the pool of
milkshake on the table.

The reporter seemed to
finally come to his senses.
He jumped up.

'Stretcher!' he shouted.
'Ambulance! Fire brigade!
Escaped-monkey catcher!'

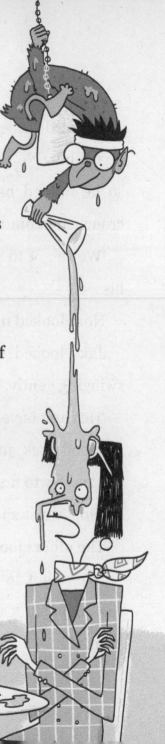

A crowd gathered round Mrs Blunt, trying to revive her. No one paid any attention to Jake, so he limped back to where the others were crouched behind the table.

'We've got to get Creature out of here,' Jake hissed.

Nora looked up. 'He's gone!'

Jake looked too. All he saw was the light, swinging gently.

'He can't have gone far . . .'

Woodstock jumped up. 'Everyone—spread out and try to find him!'

'No.' Alexis spoke for the first time in ages.

The others looked at her.

'We've got to get ready for the semi-finals,' she snapped. 'Creature will have to look after himself.'

Jake shook his head. 'Creature *can't* look after himself! You know what he's like—he'll get in all kinds of trouble.'

Nora nodded. 'I agree. Getting Mr Hyde back safe and sound is more important than winning a football game.'

Alexis put her hands on her hips. 'I'm the captain! You have to do what I say!'

'You sounded just like Amelia then,' Karl said. Alexis went bright red, and opened her mouth to retort.

*This is no good,* Jake thought. 'Guys, stop it! This isn't getting us anywhere . . .' Suddenly, out of the corner of his eye, he saw the chocolate machine shaking. He nudged Nora.

'What's that machine doing?'

A pair of sticky, furry legs was poking out

of the drawer at the bottom of the machine, thrashing madly.

'It's Creature—he's stuck!' Karl said.

Jake ran over and started pulling Creature's legs.

'Wait—you'll hurt him,' Nora said. She hurried over and they gently eased Creature out of the drawer. He flailed about like an enraged eel, then went limp.

'He's faking,' Karl said, but then there was a loud, snotty snore.

Jake grinned. 'He's asleep!'

Woodstock ran over with a tablecloth.

'Here ...' They wrapped the snoring Creature up in the cloth.

Jake turned to Alexis. 'See—he can't look after himself!'

Alexis shrugged. 'Anyway, he's safe now. So let's get on with the business of winning this tournament!'

# CHAPTER 6

## TEAM FURY AT BANANA KIT MIX-UP!

With the sleeping Creature wrapped in the tablecloth, they raced out of the café into the club house lobby, just opposite the changing rooms, as a voice came over the tannoy.

'FIFTEEN MINUTES TO KICK-OFF!'

'We need to change into the new kits,' Alexis said, opening the door to the girls' changing room. 'Oh—Amelia! What's wrong?'

Amelia was standing there, kitbag in hand and a grim look on her face.

'See for yourself!'

Everyone crowded round. Jake hung back— he couldn't let Amelia see Creature. Looking round, he spotted a big locker unit. *Perfect!* He carefully slid the sleeping Creature into an empty locker, and closed the door. When he turned back, Amelia was pulling a yellow kit out of the bag.

*Our kits aren't yellow,* Jake thought.

'These aren't kits!' Alexis cried. 'They're banana costumes!'

'Yes,' Amelia said. 'Who would play such a nasty trick?'

'What makes you think it was deliberate?' Karl asked.

Amelia smirked. 'I don't want to blame anyone, but *Barnaby* gave me the bag.'

Jake glared at her. 'Barnaby wouldn't do that to us!' But as he spoke, a memory popped into his head. *What had Alexis said to Barnaby earlier? 'I'd never be seen dead in a banana costume!' And Barnaby was angry about being a banana. Could he have done this to get Alexis back?* Reluctantly, he told the others his suspicions.

Alexis looked ready to explode. 'It must have been Barnaby!'

'Let's find him and get the proper kits back!' Woodstock cried.

Alexis shook her head. 'No time. We'll have to wear these.'

She disappeared with Amelia into the girls'

changing room. Jake, Karl, and Woodstock went into the boys' changing room, and pulled on the banana costumes. They filed back into the lobby. After a minute, Alexis and Amelia appeared in full banana regalia.

Five bananas looked at each other silently.

'We look ridiculous,' Karl said, finally. 'I'm not playing in this.'

'Me neither,' Woodstock said, slumping down on a bench.

'At least they're the right size,' Jake said, trying to lighten the mood. It didn't work. There was another gloomy silence.

Suddenly, Alexis spoke. 'Listen, everyone. I don't want to wear a banana costume either.' She raised her voice. 'But this isn't about how we look. It's about going onto that pitch and giving it our all!'

Everyone stared at Alexis. There was fire in her eyes.

'Who cares if people laugh?' she cried. 'We will see this to the end! We will play in oversized shirts, we will play in humungous shorts . . . we will play in banana costumes, we will NEVER SURRENDER!!!!'

Woodstock jumped up. 'Yeah!'

'Let's do it!' Karl shouted, punching the air.

'WHAT ARE WE?' Alexis yelled.

'WINNERS!!!!' they roared back.

'Weirdos, more like,' Jake heard Amelia mutter from behind him. He turned, but felt a sudden stab of pain in his ankle. Nora looked at him, concerned.

'You can't play with your ankle, Jake!'

Jake started to protest, but Alexis nodded. 'Nora's right,

Jake. We'll bring on Ralph—'

'ALL PLAYERS TO PITCH SIDE!' barked the loudspeaker.

'Woodstock, grab a kit for Ralph. Time to play ball!'

Alexis marched out, followed by Karl, Woodstock, and Amelia. The door slammed shut, leaving Nora and Jake alone in the suddenly quiet lobby.

RATTLE.

Nora froze. 'What was that?'

RATTLE.

'I don't know,' Jake said, looking round.

RAT-AT-AT-AT-AT-AT-AT-AT-ATTLE!!!!

The locker unit was rocking backwards and forwards as if possessed. Jake jumped up.

'Creature!'

He ran to the locker and opened the door, just in time to catch Creature as he rocketed out. At the same moment, Jake heard voices outside the club house door.

'Someone's coming!'

'Quick!' Nora disappeared into the girls' changing room. Jake hesitated, but Nora's arm shot back out and yanked him in. 'It's OK—no one's in here.'

In the nick of time! As the door swung closed, Creature squirmed out of Jake's arms, hurled himself at a coat hook and swung round it three times before launching himself up to the ceiling. He landed on a beam and perched there, picking soggy chips out of his fur and flinging them down. One landed in Nora's hair.

'Stop it, Creature!' she exclaimed, picking it out. 'Oh, why did we let Mr Hyde get over-excited?'

'Maybe he'd change back if he got really bored,' Jake said.

Nora thought. 'Well . . . we could try teaching him the two times table. That's pretty boring.'

'You're right! Creature—repeat after me. One times two is . . .'

'Kipper,' Creature said.

'No—one times two is two,' Nora said, crossly.

'Two twos are . . .'

'**Kipper.**'

'No, four. Three twos are . . .'

'**KIPPPPPPPPERRRRRRRRR!!!**' Creature started hurling himself frantically around the changing room.

'It's making him worse!' Jake noticed a whiteboard on the wall. 'I know, you could do some match tactics stuff on the board. That's pretty bor—um—relaxing.'

Nora gave Jake a look, but she picked up the pen and started drawing.

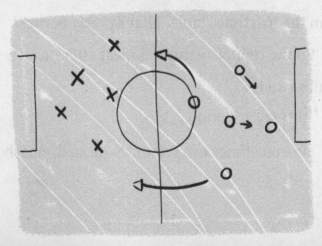

'So . . . the box formation gives a balance between attack and defence, but if the other team are strong . . .'

Jake glanced at Creature. He was staring, eyes glazed, at Nora's diagram. *Maybe it was working!*

'. . . a pyramid formation would—HEY!'

Creature snatched the pen out of Nora's hand and scribbled 'CREECHER ROOLZ' all over her diagram.

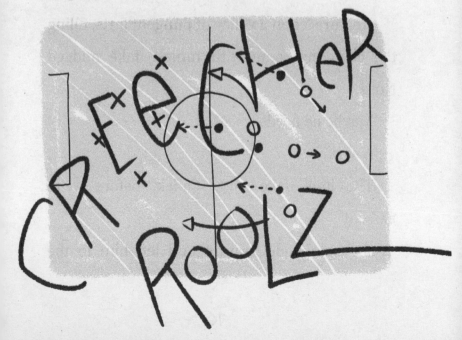

Nora grabbed the pen back. 'You've spelt that wrong.' She started writing it out again, correctly. 'C-R-E-A...'

Jake laughed. 'Never mind the spelling—'

**HONK!** A fart erupted from Creature's bottom. Three seconds later, a cabbagey pong filled the air. Jake and Nora held their noses. Creature held his too.

'Eurgh!' Jake exclaimed. 'That's gross!'

Creature let off a volley of pungent farts, filling the changing room with fumes. Jake nudged Nora.

'Maybe he needs...'

'A cork?'

'The loo!' Jake said. 'Quick, before we're gassed!'

They grabbed Creature and led him to the

toilets. Jake opened the door and shunted Creature in. He heard a cubicle door slam, then what sounded like an underwater volcano erupting.

Then silence.

'He must have finished,' Nora said.

Jake opened the toilet door. 'Creature?'

He walked in and pushed the door to each cubicle. The end one was locked.

Jake knocked. No answer. Uneasily, Jake knelt down and peered under the door.

Empty.

But a small window, high up in the wall, was wide open.

# CHAPTER 7

## TEAM CAPTAIN TAKES
## DIFFICULT DECISION

'He's gone!' Jake shouted to Nora.

'No!'

'Yes! Out the window . . .' Jake scrambled to his feet and hobbled back to the door, trying to ignore the pain in his ankle. 'Come on . . . we can't let him escape!'

He followed Nora as she ran across the changing room and out into the club house lobby. As they reached the main door, it burst open and Alexis, Karl, and Woodstock ran in, laughing and chattering. Alexis grabbed Jake and started swinging him round.

'WE WON! WE'RE THROUGH TO THE FINAL!!' she gabbled.

'Ow . . . Alexis . . . stop . . . listen . . .

Creature . . .' Jake gasped, as he whirled round and round.

Alexis let go and started swinging Nora round instead.

'2–1! What a game!' Woodstock shouted, doing a victory dance with Karl. Jake waved his hands.

'Guys, listen—'

'That last goal was awesome, Woodstock!' Karl shouted. He started singing.

'Weeeeeeeee are the champions, my frieeeeend . . .'

'PAY ATTENTION TO JAKE!' Nora shouted. Alexis, Karl, and Woodstock stopped capering about and looked at Jake.

'We need to tell you—hang on.' Jake looked round. 'Where are Amelia and Ralph?'

'Amelia broke a nail and had to be stretchered off,' Karl said.

Jake stared. 'Really?'

Woodstock giggled. 'She wasn't stretchered off, but she made such a fuss you'd think she'd broken a leg. So her darling mummy took her off to bandage her up. And Ralph went to get a banana smoothie.'

'That's good. We don't have much time,' Jake said.

Woodstock looked puzzled. 'For what?'

'Time to prepare for the next match, of course,' Alexis said, jumping up, a crazed look in her eye. 'Let's get our battle plan together—we're so close to winning now! The cup is as good as mine . . . I mean ours—'

'Actually, that wasn't what I meant,' Jake interrupted. 'Creature has escaped. We have to go and look for him—now!'

Alexis crossed her arms. 'Fine. Off you go.'

'Alexis, we need your help,' Nora said. 'You play football here every week—you're the only one of us who knows their way around.'

Jake nodded. Alexis stared at Nora, then at Jake, her cheeks flushed.

'Don't you get it?' she snapped. 'This is the most important match of my life! We HAVE to win that trophy! And we won't if we all have to go off on a wild goose chase after that stupid Creature.'

She stopped. Everyone stared at her in silence. Nora looked shocked.

'Karl was right. You really are starting to sound like Amelia.'

Before Alexis could reply, the door swung open again. A banana-clad marshal's head poked round it.

'Oh, here you are—'

'BARNABY MCCRUMB!' Alexis strode forward and dragged him inside.

'What did you do with our kits?!' she shouted.

Barnaby stared at Alexis's banana costume. His eyes flicked to Woodstock, Karl, and Jake, in theirs.

'I—'

'You swapped our kits for banana costumes!' Alexis cried.

Barnaby started to open his mouth again.

'And don't you *dare* deny it!'

Barnaby flushed cherry red. 'Fine, I won't!!'

He turned on his heel and stomped back out of the door. It was only then that Jake noticed a man standing in the doorway. He stepped neatly aside to let Barnaby through.

'Hi kids, hope I'm not interrupting anything,' the man said, jovially. 'I'm Phil, from the *Gazette*.'

Jake recognized him as the reporter they'd seen in the café with Mrs Blunt. Amelia was hovering behind him.

'I just want a little interview with the captain, if she's around,' Phil said.

Alexis took a few deep breaths. She stepped forward and showed her captain's armband proudly.

'I'm Alexis. I'm the captain.'

Amelia pushed past the reporter to stand next to Alexis. 'And I'm the deputy captain,' she said loudly.

The reporter glanced at her. 'Oh, hello.' He turned back to Alexis and held out a microphone.

'So, Alexis, how confident are you of winning today?'

'Well, Phil,' Alexis said, 'we've been training intensively—'

Suddenly, Amelia thrust her face at the microphone. 'Very confident,' she said. 'With me on the pitch, we're bound to win! I ran the other team ragged in our last game. Did you see it?'

The reporter looked at her. 'Sorry, no, I didn't. What do you think, Alexis?'

'Well, we've got a really strong game plan, thanks to—'

'Thanks to me, we won the last two games!' Amelia interrupted. 'I set up those two goals single-handedly! I'm a natural footballer. Just ask Daddy . . .'

'Actually, that's not—' Alexis began, but Amelia grabbed the microphone off the reporter and turned so that Alexis couldn't reach it.

'You know, Daddy is one of the sponsors today. He owns Burt's Banana Smoothies. But anyway, let's talk about me . . .'

Alexis tried again. 'It's working as a team that's important—'

But Amelia butted in again and drowned her out. 'Personality is the most important thing . . . the cup is as good as mine . . . I mean ours—'

Alexis made a sudden, strangled noise in her throat. Jake looked at her. She was staring at Amelia as though she'd seen a ghost. It suddenly hit Jake why—Alexis had said exactly the same words a few minutes before!

Jake heard Amelia declaring, 'It's all about winning . . .'

'RIGHT! That's it!'

A pale-faced Alexis ripped off her captain's armband. Everyone stared at her. The reporter raised his eyebrows and scribbled something in his notebook.

'What are you doing?' Woodstock asked, astonished.

Alexis looked at Amelia. 'It's not *all* about winning. Winning is great, but—' she looked over at Nora and Jake—'supporting your friends and being there for them is more important.'

She swallowed hard and held the armband out to Amelia. 'You want to win so much—here, have this. I resign the captaincy. You're the captain now, Amelia.'

# CHAPTER 8

## COMMENTATOR ATTACKED BY GIANT BANANAS!

A triumphant look crept over Amelia's face. She grabbed the armband from Alexis and put it on, just as an announcement came over the tannoy—the final was about to start!

'Right, we've got a match to win!' Amelia turned to the confused reporter. 'I'm captain now—so you'll want some photos of me,' she said, taking his arm and dragging him out of the club house. 'Make sure you get my best side . . .'

'Karl, Woodstock—you'd better go too,' Alexis said, as Amelia and the reporter disappeared.

'Aren't you going to play at all, then?' Woodstock asked.

Alexis shook her head. 'Like you guys said: I have to help look for Creature. You'll need to take a kit for Oliver.'

She gave Karl the last banana costume, and he and Woodstock reluctantly trooped off. Alexis watched them go, then heaved a big sigh. Nora put an arm round her shoulders.

'Alexis, you didn't have to . . .'

'I did. I *was* starting to sound like Amelia. I'm not like her really, am I?'

Jake shook his head. 'No. You just proved
that.'

Alexis stood tall.

'Well, we can't hang around—we've got a
Creature to catch!'

Jake slapped his forehead. 'Of course! Come on . . .'

Outside, the crowd was moving as one towards the main pitch, ready for the final. Dotted around in the crowd, Jake could see the bobbing tops of the marshals' banana costumes, and a band was playing. It was like being at a carnival.

Nora pulled a face. 'How will we find him in this crowd?'

'It shouldn't be hard,' Jake said. 'He usually leaves a trail of chaos behind him.'

As they peered around, trying to spot a trail of chaos, a nearby loudspeaker crackled on. Jake was expecting a 'five minutes to kick off' type announcement. So he was very surprised to hear a familiar voice sing out . . .

'KIP-KIP-KIP-KIP-KIPPERRRRR! KIP-A-KIPPER-KIP-KIP-PERRRRRRRRRR!'

Nora, Jake and Alexis stared at each other.

'Creature!' Jake grabbed Alexis. 'He must be in the commentator's box! Where is it?'

'The other end of the main pitch—come on!'

Alexis started running, followed by Nora. Still limping, Jake tried to keep them in sight as they dodged through the crowds lining the pitch.

'KIP-KIP-KIP-KIP-KIPPERRRRR!' came Creature's voice again over the tannoy. Jake could see people in the crowd looking at each other in confusion.

'Maybe "Kippers" is the other team's nickname?' he heard someone say.

'No—they're the Bananas! Hello, here's an

escaped banana!'

Jake felt his face burning as people laughed and pointed at him, but he said nothing, and limped on. As the whistle blew for kick-off, a chant went round their team's supporters, on the other side of the pitch.

'COME ON, YOU BANANAS!'

Ahead, Alexis was beckoning urgently. 'Jake! Up here . . .'

A flight of steps led up to a low building with glass windows along the front. As they reached the top of the steps, Jake saw a short, black-haired man outside, banging furiously on the door. His face was blown up like an angry puffer fish, and he was holding a large strawberry milkshake in one hand.

'Some joker's locked me out!' he burst out.

'And now they're making stupid noises into the microphone. Everyone'll think it's me!' He hammered on the door again.

'Let me in, you loony, or I'm calling the police!'

' BU-U-U-UUUUUUUUURRRRRRRRRRRRRR RRRRRRRRRRRRRR-R-R-R-R-R-P!'

One of Creature's record-breakingly long burps reverberated around the sports club. Jake saw the sea of heads below him turn to look up at the commentator's box. He pulled Alexis and Nora to one side.

'What now?' he muttered.

'There's usually a window open round the back,' Alexis whispered. 'Follow me ...'

Leaving the commentator banging fruitlessly away on the door, Jake and Nora followed

Alexis to the rear of the building. Sure enough, a window was open, just big enough to climb through. Jake gave Alexis a leg-up. It was touch and go for a minute, as her banana costume caught on the window latch, but she made it. She grabbed Jake's hand and yanked him up.

'Ouch! My ankle . . .'

'Sorry!'

Jake eased himself through, trying not to bash his sore

ankle on the window frame.

'Stupid banana costumes!' he said, as his costume also caught on the window latch. 'We should have taken them off . . .'

He finally unhooked himself and lowered himself down into a small kitchen area, with a door on the other side. As Alexis pulled Nora through the window, Jake tiptoed over to the door and turned the handle.

Squeeeeeeee-e-e-eak!

'Jake!' Alexis hissed. 'Creature will hear! I'll do it . . .'

Alexis carefully turned the handle and pushed the door open a crack.

'I think I can see him,' she whispered.

Jake peeked through. He saw a long desk in front of the big windows that looked out onto the pitches. In front of this was a large leather swivel chair. It was facing away from him but over the chair back, he could see Creature's scruffy shock of dark hair.

'I'll go this side, Jake—you go the other,' Alexis whispered. 'Nora, get ready to grab him if he manages to escape . . .'

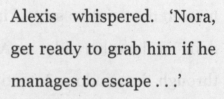

Quiet as mice (the non-squeaking variety), they tiptoed towards the chair. Closer . . . closer . . .

'GOTCHA!' Alexis shouted. As she hurled herself round the chair and grabbed Creature, Jake did the same on his side.

There was a terrified howl. But it wasn't a Creature howl.

It wasn't Creature's shock of black hair they'd seen over the chair back.

It was the commentator's!

Jake and Alexis jumped back as if they'd been burned. Nora was still behind the chair and couldn't see anything.

'What's the matter?!' she cried.

Before anyone could say or do anything, the commentator grabbed the microphone.

'MURDER! ROBBERY! I'M BEING ATTACKED BY GIANT BANANAS!'

# CHAPTER 9

## TEAM CAPTAIN IN RUCKUS WITH REF!

'MURDER! ROBBERY! I'M BEING ATTACKED BY GIANT BANANAS!' The commentator's words reverberated around the grounds.

Out of the window, Jake saw a sea of startled faces below swivel to look up at the commentator's box. Some people even started to run towards it.

Jake's brain went into overdrive. He

grabbed the microphone from the gibbering commentator and spoke in the deepest voice he could muster.

'I MEAN THE . . . THE BANANAS ARE REALLY MURDERING THE OPPOSITION . . . UM, IT'S LIKE DAYLIGHT ROBBERY . . . AND I'M REALLY ADMIRING THE ATTACKING TACTICS OF THE BANANAS TODAY!'

It was strange to hear his own voice ringing out across the stadium, ten times louder than it usually was! Jake watched anxiously, and breathed a sigh of relief as the faces below slowly turned away again, back to the match.

'Give me that!' The commentator seized the microphone from Jake. 'What are you lot playing at? Nearly gave me a blimmin' heart attack!'

'We're really sorry,' Alexis said. 'We were trying to catch that, um, joker—the one who locked you out. What happened to him?'

The commentator pointed to the door.

'He left, but only after burping in my face, knocking my milkshake over, and then running off between my legs! A kid dressed as a monkey—*whatever next?* And then you lot show up dressed as blimmin' bananas. The world's gone mad!' The commentator glared at Jake. 'So he's in your gang, is he? I'm going to have to report this.' He grabbed a pen and notebook. 'What are your names?'

Alexis threw Jake a scared look.

'I haven't got all day! What's your name, boy?'

Not knowing what else to do, Jake opened his mouth to speak, when Nora gave a cry.

'Something's happening on the pitch!'

The commentator whipped round. Jake and Alexis ran to the window.

Down on the pitch, Jake could see Amelia yelling at the referee, while the rest of the players crowded round, waving their arms.

The commentator grabbed the microphone and started talking very fast into it.

'WELL, LOOKS LIKE THE REF AWARDED A FREE KICK JUST OUTSIDE THE BOX BUT

THERE'S SOME KIND OF DISPUTE OVER
WHO'S GOING TO TAKE IT—THE CAPTAIN
OF THE BANANAS IS GOING BANANAS! I
CAN'T BEGIN TO GUESS WHAT SHE JUST
SAID TO THE REF . . .'

'Amelia's causing trouble,' Alexis said. 'She'll
get sent off if she's not careful. We can't afford
to lose a player now!'

'. . . IT'S A BOOKING, FOR SURE . . .'

The ref pulled out a yellow card and held it
up to Amelia.

'YELLOW CARD—I THINK THE CAPTAIN'S
GOING TO APPEAL . . . BUT NO, WHAT'S
HAPPENING NOW? SHE'S RUNNING BACK TO
THE BALL, AND—OH DEAR!—SHE'S KICKED
THE BALL AWAY. A CASE OF SOUR GRAPES,
I THINK . . .'

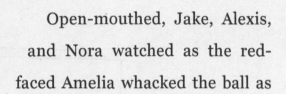

Open-mouthed, Jake, Alexis, and Nora watched as the red-faced Amelia whacked the ball as hard as she could towards the goal. But she sliced it, and, instead of rocketing straight into the net, it soared off towards the sideline in a graceful curve.

'THERE'S A BANANA KICK IF EVER I SAW ONE!' the commentator cried.

'Tsk,' Nora tutted. 'Terrible angle!'

The ball flew towards the crowd.

Jake stared. 'It's going to hit someoooooooooooooone . . . . . . . . .'

THWACK!

It hit a tall woman smack on the back of the head. Even from a distance, Jake could see who it was. There was no mistaking that black, sharply bobbed hair, although it was looking slightly pinker than usual after the strawberry milkshake incident.

'Mrs Blunt!' Alexis said, covering her mouth.

'Ooh, I can't look,' Nora said, but she did.

Mrs Blunt staggered drunkenly, flailed her arms around, then sank in a heap on the ground.

From up in the box, Jake saw the crowd go completely still.

But only for a second. Jake couldn't hear much, but he saw people waving, and their mouths opening and closing, as if he was watching a film with the sound turned down. A first-aid team raced up and disappeared into the crowd. A minute later they emerged, with Mrs Blunt on a stretcher.

Jake felt a nudge in his ribs.

'Let's go,' Nora said, quietly. 'Before *he* notices . . .'

She rolled her eyes towards the commentator, who was still gabbling away at top speed. He seemed to have forgotten about Jake, Alexis, and Nora, who tiptoed out quietly. As the door closed behind him, Jake felt something sticky underfoot.

'Ugh, what's that?!' he exclaimed, looking

down. He'd stepped in a puddle of gooey pink stuff.

'Milkshake!' Nora said. 'I stepped in it too. Creature spilt it, didn't he . . .'

'Look!' Alexis pointed. Leading away from the puddle of milkshake at the door was a trail of strawberry pink pawprints.

Jake laughed. 'Creature got covered in milkshake—again! This should be easy . . .'

They followed the pawprints down the steps, then back past the pitches towards the club house. The prints got fainter and fainter. Finally, they disappeared completely.

Alexis scratched her head. 'Which way now?'

They were standing next to a small white tent with a red cross on it. Inside, Jake could hear someone talking in a loud voice.

'It's very white in here. Is this the White House? So you must be the President. Wonderful to meet you, Your Presidentness!'

'That's Mrs Blunt!' Nora said. 'What's she wittering on about?'

They crept to the door of the tent and listened.

'You're very small. I always thought the President would be bigger!'

Jake suppressed a snort of laughter. 'That knock sent her silly in the head,' he whispered to Nora and Alexis.

Mrs Blunt's voice was getting more and more muffled, for some reason.

'I must say, you have extremely hairy hands, Mr President.'

Jake, Alexis, and Nora stared at each other.

'Could it—no it couldn't possibly be . . . ?'

# CHAPTER 10

## HEAD'S BRAINS ADDLED AFTER ALIEN ABDUCTION

'Hairy hands?' Nora breathed in Jake's ear. 'You don't think . . .'

Jake peered through the tent flap—then jerked back in shock.

An Egyptian mummy was looking silently at him.

Jake took a deep breath, then peeked again . . .

He breathed out. Egyptian mummies didn't

wear high heels. It was Mrs Blunt. And she wasn't looking at him—in fact, she couldn't see him at all because her head was completely wrapped in bandages.

On a trolley next to her sat a box from which a scuffling noise was coming. Then Creature's head popped out of it. He was winding a bandage round Mrs Blunt's head. He'd already wrapped her arms and torso.

As Jake watched, Creature got himself in a knot with the bandages. He turned round and round, getting more and more tangled up. Then, with a yelp, he fell off the trolley, pulling the box of bandages down on top of himself.

'Neeeeep!'

'Ooommmfff?' Mrs Blunt mumbled through the bandages.

'Where are all the first-aiders?' Jake heard Nora whisper from behind him.

'Gone to deal with another injury, probably,' he whispered back. Glancing around to make

sure no one was coming, he pushed the tent flap back and tiptoed into the tent.

'What are you doing?!' Alexis hissed.

'Getting Creature!' Jake skirted past the mummified Mrs Blunt, who was frantically trying to hoick her arms free.

'Oomffa-oomffa-OOMFF!' Mrs Blunt staggered to her feet, as Jake hurled himself at the upside-down bandage box . . .

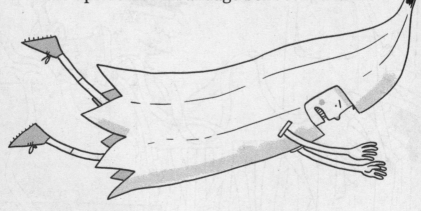

. . . and missed. He caught a glimpse of

Creature's eyes through a slit in the box, before it bolted towards the tent door, a trail of bandages billowing out behind it.

'OOMFFA-OOMFFA-OOMFF!' Mrs Blunt's "oomffs" were getting more panicky.

'Stop that box!' Jake shouted, seeing Nora and Alexis's faces staring through the tent flap. Nora made a grab for it, but the box veered the other way . . .

**CR-R-R-RASH!!** It careered into a trolley piled with medical supplies. Over went the

trolley, in an avalanche of boxes and bottles. Creature's box shot out from under the trolley, straight into Mrs Blunt's legs.

'Ooooomfffff!!' Mrs Blunt oomffed again. The box ran in circles round her legs, wrapping them in trailing bandages, with Jake in hot pursuit. Mrs Blunt tried to step forward. But her ankles were now tightly bound. She tripped and toppled . . .

'Got you!' Alexis and Nora ran forward and caught the falling headteacher, as Jake flung himself on top of the runaway box.

'Eeeee! Eeeee!' The box shook Jake till his teeth rattled, but he held on grimly.

Finally it went still.

Jake peeked cautiously through the slit. Inside, Creature was slumped, panting. He looked thoroughly pooped.

Nora and Alexis unwound Mrs Blunt, from the toes up. Finally, her eyes appeared, blinking in the light. Her voice wobbled a bit as she spoke.

'Why it's Nora, isn't it? And—let me see—Alexis, and Jake! Thank you for rescuing me, my dear children . . .'

Alexis, Nora, and Jake looked at each other, at a loss for words. What had got into Mrs Blunt? She never had a nice word to say to anyone!

There was a rustle at the tent door.

'How are you doing—hey, what's going on here?'

A white-coated woman was standing in the doorway, looking at them in astonishment.

Mrs Blunt stepped forward. 'Let me explain, doctor. I was just lying on the couch here, having a nice chat with the President of the United States, when aliens came down and wrapped me in some kind of cocoon . . .'

The first-aider clucked her tongue.

'I think you'd better lie down,' she said. 'You must have concussion! Let me see that bump . . .' She bustled the headteacher back to the couch. 'And you children, out now, please!'

Grabbing the box with Creature in, Jake ducked out of the tent. As Nora and Alexis appeared behind him, a shrill whistle blew over at the main pitch.

'It's half-time,' Alexis said. 'Shall we go and see what's happening? And then take Creature back to the changing rooms?'

Jake peeked into the box. 'He's asleep. OK, but we'll have to be quick.'

As they approached the pitch, Jake saw a bunch of bedraggled bananas trudging glumly off. To his surprise, he saw that there were only three players—Amelia, Woodstock, and the last sub, Oliver.

Amelia threw herself on the ground dramatically.

'It's hopeless!' she wailed, wiping a muddy hand across her muddy face and making it even muddier. 'We're losing 7–0!'

'7–0?' Alexis cried. 'How come? And where are Karl and Ralph?'

'Amelia kept yelling at Karl,' Woodstock said, angrily. 'So he stomped off, saying he'd rather practise the brass band's award ceremony routine. Then Ralph got poked in the eye so he had to go off too. Two of you will have to come back on.'

'What's the point?! We'll never win,' Amelia wailed from the ground. 'I don't want to be captain any more!' She crawled over and clutched Alexis's leg. 'Please, Alexis, come back

and be captain! I'm not a natural footballer, I'm much better at pony riding . . .'

Alexis patted Amelia's head awkwardly.

'You'll be fine, Amelia! You're a strong person, you can do this—'

Amelia looked up at Alexis. Her lip wobbled. Then her face crumpled and she burst into a long wailing sob.

'Waaaaaaaaaaaaaaaaah!'

The box in Jake's arms twitched. Jake clutched it more tightly and looked nervously through the slit, but Creature's eyes were still closed.

'I'm not a strong person,' Amelia howled. 'I'm a horrible person!'

Alexis rolled her eyes. 'You haven't been that bad, Amelia . . .'

Amelia scrambled to her feet, smearing mud and tears all over her face. She grabbed Alexis by the shoulders.

'You don't understand.' She stared round at everyone. 'I've done something horrid.'

There was a confused silence.

'What have you done, Amelia?' Nora finally asked.

Amelia swallowed hard.

'It wasn't Barnaby who swapped the football kits for banana costumes. It was me.'

# CHAPTER 11

## REVELATIONS OF FOUL PLAY SHOCK TEAM

'*You?* It was you who swapped our kits for banana costumes?' Alexis said, a stunned look on her face.

Amelia hung her head. 'Yes.'

There was a short, shocked silence. Jake's mind whirled. But that was impossible! *Why, he'd watched Barnaby give the bag to Amelia himself—but then she'd been in the changing*

*room on her own; she would have had time . . .*
It still didn't make sense.

'But why?' he asked. 'You knew you'd have to wear one yourself!'

Amelia stared at the ground. 'I-I thought Alexis would refuse to play wearing one. Because of what she'd said earlier—that she wouldn't be seen dead in a banana costume.'

Jake felt a sudden hot flush of guilt. *What an idiot I am!* Amelia had heard that comment as well as Barnaby. How could he have suspected Barnaby, and not Amelia?! And he'd made the others think . . . he opened his mouth, but Nora got there before him.

'You did it so you could be captain! Did you lock Alexis in the toilet too?'

Amelia nodded, biting her lip.

'I don't care much for football,' she sniffed. 'But I did want to be captain. So I asked Daddy to get me on the team. He'd just made a big donation to Mrs Blunt's Headteacher Statue Fund, so he had a word with Mrs Blunt yesterday and she put me on the team. But she wouldn't make me captain!'

Jake couldn't bear it any longer. He burst out.

'The worst thing is that you made us blame Barnaby.'

'Blame me for what?'

Jake turned, to see Barnaby standing behind him, still in his banana costume and looking extremely fed up.

'Tell him, Amelia,' Jake said.

Amelia spoke with an effort. 'I-I swapped

the kits. After you gave me the bag, I swapped the kits for banana costumes. But I made them think you did it.' She paused and cleared her throat. 'I'm, well, I'm—sorrrr-aargh.' She sort of gurgled the last word.

Barnaby stared at her. 'What?'

'Sorrr-reurgh.'

Barnaby shook his head. 'Still not getting it . . .'

'SORRY!' Amelia finally spat the word out. Jake thought she'd probably never said it in her life before.

'Apology accepted.' Barnaby grinned. 'It was quite funny. Wish I'd thought of it.'

'Barnaby!' Nora said, shocked.

Jake shook his head. 'But Barnaby—why didn't you say anything when we accused you of swapping the kits? Why didn't you say it wasn't you?'

Barnaby shrugged.

'You guys always think I'm up to no good. Everyone thinks that. You'd made up your minds it was me; you'd never have believed me if I'd said it wasn't.'

'That's not true—' Woodstock began.

Barnaby stopped him. 'It *is* true. Plus I was in a bad mood. I really wanted to play today! I'm not very good at much, but I'm pretty good at football. Finally, I had the chance to prove I could do something well for a change. And instead I had to wander around dressed as a banana, helping old people to their seats.'

'Well, we all ended up as bananas,' Woodstock said, 'and you were good at showing people to their seats. My grandad seems to like you . . .' He pointed. Jake looked along the sideline to see Woodstock's grandad waving his megaphone.

'HELLO BANANABY!!!!' he roared into it.

Barnaby winced. 'Great—I make a good banana. And old people like me.'

'It's good to be liked,' Nora said.

'Anyway, you're good at loads of stuff,' Jake said. 'That thing where you make rhythms with your mouth . . .'

'Beatboxing.' A slight smile twitched Barnaby's mouth. 'Yeah, s'pose I am.'

'And you're a great friend,' Woodstock said.

'And...'—Alexis leaned forward and whispered so that Amelia wouldn't hear—'you're really good with Creature.' She turned to the others. 'I think we should all apologize to Barnaby for suspecting him of swapping the kits.'

They all nodded. 'Sorry, Barnaby,' everyone chorused.

Just then the tannoy burst into life.

'FIVE MINUTES TO THE SECOND HALF! TEAMS, PREPARE FOR THE FINAL SHOWDOWN!'

Amelia looked pleadingly at Alexis. 'Please go on instead of me,' she begged. 'If you go on as captain, you could pull it back!'

Woodstock looked at Amelia in disgust. 'Scaredy-cat. I bet you just don't want to be on the pitch when we lose! Then you can tell everyone it wasn't your fault. We should tell Mrs Blunt what you did.'

Amelia went pale. Alexis shook her head.

'I don't think so, Woodstock. She's learned her lesson. Haven't you, Amelia?'

Amelia nodded eagerly. 'Oh yes, I have! I won't do it again, honest! Please don't tell Mrs Blunt. I'll do anything . . .'

Alexis raised her eyebrows. 'Anything?'

'Anything.'

Alexis planted her hands on her hips. 'OK. Get back out there and play some top-quality football, then.'

Amelia's face fell.

'In goal,' Alexis added.

Amelia's face fell even further. Jake grinned.

In goal was not where you wanted to be when the other team were up 7–0.

'I'll come on as captain,' Alexis said. 'But we're two players down. We need one more. Jake—how's your ankle?'

Holding the box with Creature tightly, Jake wiggled his ankle. It wasn't as bad as before, but it looked swollen.

'I think I could . . .'

'How about Barnaby?' Nora said, suddenly.

Everyone looked at Barnaby. His face lit up. 'Really?'

Alexis shrugged. 'Why not? The only reason you weren't picked was because you weren't there.'

Barnaby punched the air. 'Let me at 'em! They don't call me Barnaby Beckham Ronaldo

McRooney for nothing!'

Jake laughed. 'They don't call you that at all!'

'Right, gather round,' Alexis said. 'So the team is as follows: me and Barnaby in attack; Amelia in goal; Woodstock, you and Oliver in defence—Amelia will need as much support as she can get. But watch out for attacking opportunities. We need to get goals, and plenty of them! WHAT ARE WE?'

'WINNERS!' everyone except Amelia shouted.

'What are we, Amelia?' Alexis said, firmly.

Amelia gulped. 'Winners.'

# CHAPTER 12

## GOLDEN BALL TROPHY SWIPED!

The referee was beckoning the teams onto the pitch.

'Here goes,' Alexis said. 'Are we ready?'

Everyone nodded as the other team appeared. The captain walked up to Alexis, looked her up and down, and laughed.

'Bananas: prepare to be liquidized.'

'Made into banana custard,' said another player.

'Banana splits,' said another, and they all fell about laughing. Jake saw Alexis's fists clench, and nudged her.

'Don't let them get to you,' he muttered. 'Remember what you said earlier—who cares if they laugh?'

Alexis breathed out slowly. 'Yeah. They think we're a walkover—we'll show them!'

Nora and Jake shouted encouragement as Alexis, Woodstock, Oliver, Barnaby, and Amelia walked out onto the pitch. Suddenly, Alexis turned, and pointed excitedly towards the end of the pitch. Jake looked, and saw that a podium had been set up. On top sat a gleaming gold trophy in the shape of a football.

*The Golden Ball trophy!* He tried to give Alexis a thumbs-up, but it was hard with the box in his arms. He peeked through the slit, to see Creature snuffling a bit in his sleep. Nora looked at the box, nervously.

'Shouldn't we take him back to the changing rooms?' she asked.

'He's still asleep. Let's watch a bit of the match first.'

The crowd fell silent. Then . . .

Pheeeeeeeeeeeeeeep!

'COME ON, YOU BANANAS!'

Jake and Nora both jumped, and turned. Woodstock's grandad was sitting in a chair behind them with his megaphone, straining to see over their heads.

'I can't see,' Grandad complained. 'Do you

think you could move me forward a bit? I'd do it myself, but my hip's gone . . .'

'OK.' Jake put the box on the ground, and took hold of the chair on one side. Nora took the other. 'One, two, three—GO!'

They heaved the chair forward.

'A teensy bit further . . . just a wee bit more . . . nearly there . . .'

Bit by bit, they edged the chair forward. Finally, Grandad was happy.

'Thank you, my dears.' Then he bellowed through the megaphone, 'COME ON, YOU BANANAS!'

'At least there's nothing wrong with his voice,' Nora whispered to Jake.

Jake grinned and leaned forward to try to see what was happening on the pitch. He saw Alexis take a shot, but miss. A striker from the other team got the ball and tore back up the pitch—the defenders had all gone forward. This was a dangerous situation!

'Get ready, Amelia!' Jake yelled to Amelia,

whose knees were knocking as the striker barrelled towards her.

Nora groaned. 'She'll never save it . . .'

But then, without warning, the striker stumbled. The ball rolled harmlessly towards the goal, to be grabbed by a surprised Amelia, as the striker stood completely still, staring, transfixed, at the goal.

'Why's he stopped?' Nora exclaimed.

Jake's eyes swivelled towards the goal, and then nearly popped out of his head. He grabbed Nora. 'Look!'

On top of the goalposts, perched Creature. He was whirling something round his head. Jake couldn't quite work out what it was, but it glinted golden as it caught the sunlight.

'How did *he* get there?' Nora gasped.

Jake slapped his head. 'He must have escaped when we were moving Woodstock's grandad's chair!'

An important-looking man in a grey suit burst out of the crowd, not far from Jake.

'That mascot has stolen the Golden Ball trophy!' he boomed. 'Someone call the police!'

Jake stared. It was true—the golden thing whizzing round Creature's head was the Golden Ball trophy! Jake groaned. *This is really not what we need,* he thought. He tried to see what was happening, but it was difficult. A crowd of players had gathered around the goal, and officials were running onto the pitch. He felt Nora grab his arm.

'What's Amelia doing?!' she exclaimed.

Amelia burst out of the little huddle of

players, and started running up the pitch with the ball towards the opposite goal, now goalie-free. She reached the box, swung her leg back and kicked as hard as she could. The ball rocketed into the net. Woodstock's grandad leapt out of his chair as though he'd been shot out of a cannon.

'GOOOOOOOOOOOOOAAAAAAAAAAL!' he roared, nearly deafening Jake.

The noise startled Creature too. He teetered wildly on the crossbar for a few seconds, still clutching the trophy, then fell off— POLOLLOP!—straight into a muddy puddle.

Several players tried to leap on him, but he was covered in mud and slipped through their fingers. He dashed along the goal line, still clutching the now rather mud-splattered

Golden Ball trophy. As he ran past a hotdog
stand, a man in a chef's hat and apron ran out,
waving a spatula.

'Oi! That's the blighter who dive-bombed into my ketchup!'

The man started running after Creature. Two banana-clad marshals joined him. Jake saw that they were carrying a large net, and a sudden, horrible vision of a terrified Creature in a cage sprang to his mind.

'We can't let them catch him,' he hissed to Nora. 'They'll find out he's not a kid at all—and then who knows what they'll do to him?!'

Nora pointed. 'He's coming this way—let's try and grab him!'

Creature had swerved round the corner and was bolting down the sideline towards them. On the pitch, the game was back in full swing. Jake heard a roar from the crowd—but he had to focus on catching Creature . . .

Creature got nearer . . . and nearer . . . Jake prepared to pounce . . .

'GOTCHA!'

Just down the sideline, the important-looking man who had wanted to call the police jumped out in front of Creature. At the same moment, the two marshals skidded up with their net.

'GOTCHA!' They hurled the net at Creature.

'Noooooooo!' Jake and Nora cried, together.

# CHAPTER 13

## THEY THINK IT'S ALL OVER . . .

As if in slow motion, the net came down . . .

But the marshals had not reckoned on anyone but Creature being under it.

'AAARRRGHHH!!!!!'

The net fell over the important-looking man, trapping him.

'WAARRGHHH!!!!!!'

Unable to stop himself, the hotdog-stand man

slammed into the marshals, who fell on top of the net. As they all lay there thrashing and yelling, Jake saw Creature's face appear at the bottom of the pile-up. With a wriggle, he squirmed out from under the net and sped off, kippering triumphantly.

Jake was ready. Quick as lightning, he held out the open box and Creature hurtled straight into it. He slammed the lid shut just as the final whistle blew.

Pheeeeeeeeeeeeeeeep!

'It's a draw!' Nora cried.

Jake stared at the scoreboard. '7–7? How . . .?'

'JAKE!' Alexis came panting up. 'It's a golden goal knockout—first team to score wins! But Oliver's injured—you'll *have* to come back on . . .'

Jake shoved the box at Nora.

'Take this.' He ran onto the pitch.

'But your ankle—' Nora shouted.

'It's fine—just look after Creature!' He reached Alexis. 'How did you get seven goals?' he asked.

Alexis shrugged. 'I guess they thought we'd never catch up, so they didn't even start trying till the last five minutes. Plus we played really well! Now, let's talk tactics . . .'

She beckoned everyone round.

'We need to work as a team—pass the ball, don't hold on to it, and focus on getting that goal . . .'

'Teams to positions!' The ref put the whistle to his lips.

Pheeeeeeeeeeeeeep!

No sooner had the whistle blown than Alexis passed the ball to Jake. He caught it on his foot, and ran towards the goal. Too late, he spotted a defender coming up . . . the player hooked the ball from Jake and whacked it back up the pitch to one of his teammates, right in front of the goal!

THWACK!

'Noooooo!' In horror, Jake watched the ball curve towards the goal—but at the last second, Amelia made a superhuman leap and punched the ball away.

Woodstock cheered.

'Great save!'

'Play on,' the ref called. Alexis got to the ball and crossed it to Woodstock, who passed to Jake. Jake flicked the ball past a

defender, then crossed it back to Alexis. Barnaby hovered outside the goal box as Alexis thundered up the pitch. The goalie crouched, ready. Jake knew Alexis wanted to take the shot. But two defenders were closing in . . .

'Barnaby!' Alexis shouted, and volleyed the ball towards the far corner of the goal.

The goalie dived. But as the ball sailed past Barnaby, he took a flying leap, and headed it into the opposite corner of the net.

'GOOOOOOOAAAAAAAL!!!!!!!' roared the crowd. Barnaby had scored the golden goal! He sank to his knees.

'We did it—oommmff!'

Jake, Alexis, Amelia, and Woodstock leapt on Barnaby, hoisted him onto their shoulders, and carried him on a victory lap round the pitch. As they came to where Nora was standing, Woodstock's grandad bellowed into his megaphone.

'WEEEEEE ARE THE CHAMPIONS . . .'

'You were awesome!' Nora shouted.

'Thanks!' Jake grinned, then looked round. 'Nora—where's the box?'

'I gave it to Woodstock's grandad—' Nora's hand flew to her mouth. 'Noooo . . .'

Jake looked at Grandad. The box was still on his lap—so why was Nora scared?

Then he realized.

An orange glow was coming from inside the box. It got brighter and brighter. Amelia's mouth dropped open.

'THAT BOX IS ON FIRE!' she shouted.

Too late, Jake hurled himself at the box—

FAAAAAAAAAAAAAARRRRRRT!

Wheeeeeeee . . . . . . . . . . . .

POP! POP! POP!

BANG!

Everyone dived for cover as a cloud of purple smoke erupted around them. Jake heard shouts, and could just see Grandad through the fog, still in his chair, flapping his arms and coughing.

Not just Grandad . . . Jake wafted smoke away.

'Mr Hyde!'

A slightly steaming Mr Hyde was sitting on Grandad's lap, looking extremely surprised.

Grandad looked dazed. Then his eyes lit up and he grabbed Mr Hyde by the wrists.

'You must be a genie,' he exclaimed. 'Can you grant me a wish?'

'I'm sorry, sir, but I'm not a genie,' Mr Hyde said, trying to extricate himself from Grandad's grip.

'Grandad, this is our teacher, Mr Hyde,' Woodstock said. 'Please let him go.'

Reluctantly Grandad did so, and Mr Hyde stood up quickly. Amelia crawled out from under a chair and looked around. She stared at Mr Hyde, a puzzled frown on her face.

'How . . . what . . . why . . . ?'

'Just one of Grandad's smoke bombs,' Woodstock said, quickly. 'Look—your parents are over there, Amelia. They probably want another photograph . . .'

With one last confused look at Mr Hyde, Amelia ran off, nearly bumping into a crowd of marshals who were marching towards the podium. At their head was the important-looking man who had been trapped under the net. He was clutching the rather muddy Golden Ball trophy to his chest as if he thought it might vanish at any moment. Jake realized with a shock of excitement that the trophy now belonged to *them!* In ten minutes' time, they'd be standing on that podium.

Alexis tugged at Mr Hyde's sleeve.

'Sir, we won!' she said. 'Did you see Barnaby's amazing goal?'

'How could he? He was in the box,' Barnaby said. Mr Hyde slapped him on the back.

'Actually, I did—through the slit,' he said. 'It was brilliant, seeing you guys doing some great teamwork out there. And when Barnaby scored, I thought I would explode from pride.'

'And then you did!' Nora laughed.

Mr Hyde grinned. 'Yes, I suppose I did, didn't I?' He scratched his head. 'I do have one question, though. Why on earth are you all dressed as bananas?'

'It's a long story,' Jake said. 'But after you changed, everything sort of went a bit . . . a bit . . .'

'Pear-shaped?' Mr Hyde asked.

Jake, Alexis, Barnaby, Nora, and Woodstock all spoke at the same time.

'BANANAS!'

# Football cards

Why don't you copy and cut out these football cards, then you can play Creature Teacher top trumps!

## NORA

**Strength:** 11
**Speed:** 24
**Skill:** 42
**Tactics:** 100
**Passion:** 21
**Fair play:** 90

## BARNABY

**Strength:** 81
**Speed:** 83
**Skill:** 95
**Tactics:** 33
**Passion:** 61
**Fair play:** 48

**JAKE**

Strength: 66
Speed: 10 (due to injury)
Skill: 72
Tactics: 69
Passion: 76
Fair play: 82

**ALEXIS**

Strength: 74
Speed: 92
Skill: 98
Tactics: 75
Passion: 100
Fair play: 75

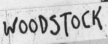

## WOODSTOCK

**Strength:** 68
**Speed:** 65
**Skill:** 66
**Tactics:** 58
**Passion:** 54
**Fair play:** 70

## KARL

**Strength:** 71
**Speed:** 52
**Skill:** 61
**Tactics:** 38
**Passion:** 57
**Fair play:** 67

**AMELIA**

Strength: 4
Speed: 29
Skill: 2
Tactics: 54
Passion: 12
Fair play: 15

**CREATURE**

Strength: 99
Speed: 99
Skill: 5
Tactics: 0
Passion: 99
Fair play: 0

# More Creature Teacher books, out now!

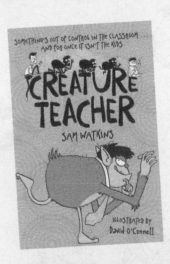

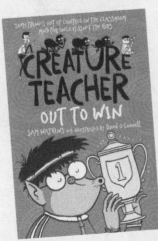

# Creature Teacher

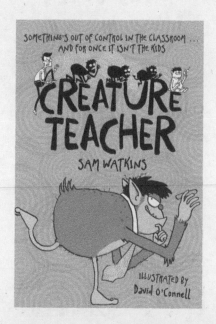

SOMETHING'S OUT OF CONTROL IN THE CLASSROOM...
AND FOR ONCE IT ISN'T THE KIDS

**CREATURE TEACHER**

SAM WATKINS

ILLUSTRATED BY
David O'Connell

Jake's class finally have the best teacher
in the world—Mr Hyde.

There is just one teeny, tiny, HUGE problem.
He transforms into a naughty little creature
whenever he becomes upset. The creature has some
amazing abilities but being well-behaved isn't one
of them! Jake and his friends will have to work as
a team to hide the creature, so they can keep their
teacher. But their headmistress, Mrs Blunt, is never
far off the scent . . .

# Creature Teacher
# Goes Wild

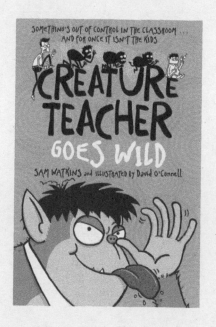

Jake's class is going to the opening of Wilf's
Wild Adventure Theme Park. The theme park
has some amazing rides—but things start to get
really WILD when their favourite teacher,
Mr Hyde, ends up turning into Creature and causing
chaos on the Ghost Train!

Will Jake and his friends be able to track down
Creature and get him to change back into Mr Hyde
before the truth about their teacher gets out?

It's going to be a roller coaster of an adventure!

# Creature Teacher
# Science Shocker

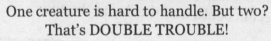

One creature is hard to handle. But two?
That's DOUBLE TROUBLE!

Jake's class are competing in the Whizz-BANG
Science Fair and surely nothing can stop them
from winning at the final. Well, maybe one thing . . .
their teacher, Mr Hyde, has turned into Creature,
and is more interested in eating the exhibits than
talking about them. And what's more,
Creature's made a friend! With two mischievous
monsters causing havoc, things are
about to get EXPLOSIVE!

## About the author

Sam Watkins voraciously consumed books from a young age, due to a food shortage in the village where she grew up. This diet, although not recommended by doctors, has given her a lifelong passion for books. She has been a bookseller, editor and publisher, and writes and illustrates her own children's books. At one point, things all got a bit too bookish so she decided to be an art teacher for a while, but books won the day in the end.

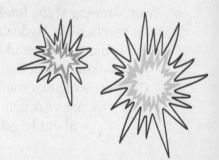

David O'Connell is an illustrator who lives in London. His favourite things to draw are monsters, naughty children (another type of monster), batty old ladies, and evil cats . . . Oh, and teachers that transform into naughty little creatures!

Here are some other stories
that we think you'll love.

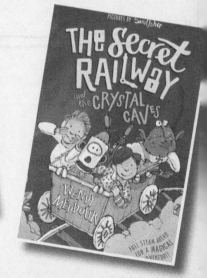